dick bruna

on my scooter

Tate Publishing

I'm off to do some scooting

I know just where to go

I'll scoot to pete the donkey

to say a quick hello

oh look at all the birds there

as I scoot on my way

and see them fly up in the air

I've scared them all away

I'm scooting very fast now

because it's quite a way

before you reach the little field

where pete the donkey stays

but now I've almost made it

I see pete look my way

he doesn't look too happy

pete, is everything ok?

why do you look so sad?

is something wrong with you?

are you not feeling very well?

have you caught the flu?

I put my scooter on the ground

and run right up to pete

perhaps he's feeling hungry

and needs some food to eat

so now I'm scooting off again

as quickly as I can -

and that is very quickly -

to john the veggie man

oh look there, I can see him

have you got a carrot, john?

oh yes, says john, I've plenty

no john, I want just one

with the carrot in my bag

I head back to pete at speed

this bag has been so handy

exactly what I need

john has some lovely carrots

quite long and really thick

I seek the very best out

and that's the one I pick

I then jump off my scooter

and run quickly back to pete

I think he's seen already

that I've something good to eat

the carrot is delicious

he's loving every crunch

I knew pete wasn't ill at all

he had just wanted lunch

Other Dick Bruna books available from Tate Publishing:

the apple 2013
I can count 2012
miffy the artist 2008
my vest is white 2012
round, square, triangle 2012
the school 2013

Published 2013 by order of the Tate Trustees
by Tate Publishing, a division of Tate Enterprises Ltd,
Millbank, London SW1P 4RG
www.tate.org.uk/publishing

Based on the original translation © copyright Patricia Crampton, 2010
This edition © Tate 2013

Original edition: *op de step*
Original text Dick Bruna © copyright Mercis Publishing bv, 2010
Illustrations Dick Bruna © copyright Mercis bv, 2010
Publication licensed by Mercis Publishing bv, Amsterdam
Printed by Sachsendruck Plauen GmbH, Germany
All rights reserved.

A catalogue record for this book is available from the British Library
ISBN 978 1 84976 216 8

Distributed in the United States and Canada by ABRAMS, New York
Library of Congress Control Number: applied for

MIX
From responsible sources
FSC® C021195
FSC
www.fsc.org